The Adventures of Commander

Zack Proton

and the
Red Giant

The Adventures of Commander Zack Proton and the Red Giant

The Adventures of Commander Zack Proton and the Warlords of Nibblecheese
(coming soon)

The Adventures of Commander Zack Proton
and the Red Giant

By Brian Anderson
Illustrated by Doug Holgate

Aladdin Paperbacks
New York · London · Toronto · Sydney

To my three squirrels: Amy, Kerry, and Linda —B. A.

For Mum, Dad, and my brother, Michael —D. H.

ALADDIN PAPERBACKS
An imprint of Simon & Schuster Children's Publishing Division
1230 Avenue of the Americas, New York, NY 10020
Text copyright ©2006 by Brian Anderson
Illustrations copyright ©2006 by Doug Holgate
All rights reserved, including the right of
reproduction in whole or in part in any form.
ALADDIN PAPERBACKS and colophon are
trademarks of Simon & Schuster, Inc.
Designed by Sammy Yuen
The text of this book was set in Zolano Serif BTN.
Manufactured in the United States of America
First Aladdin Paperbacks edition June 2006
2 4 6 8 10 9 7 5 3 1
Library of Congress Control Number 2005930116
ISBN-13: 978-1-4169-1364-1
ISBN-10: 1-4169-1364-5

CONTENTS

CHAPTER ONE

Out of the Flying Pan

Commander Zack Proton kept a watchful eye on the stars and galaxies whizzing past his window as his intergalactic starship raced toward the far end of the universe.

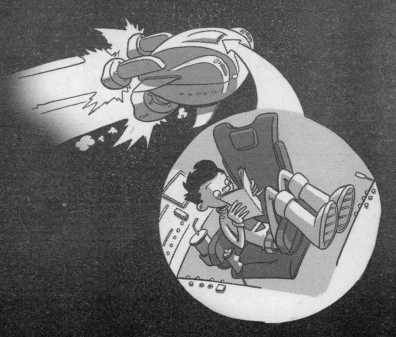

Zack was leading his squadron of space rangers on a mission to the outer-most planet of the outermost star of the outermost galaxy, with a cargo of sixteen million bags of first-class mail. People who live in the most distant corners of the universe don't get mail very often, but when they do, it's a whole stamp collection at a time.

MR & MRS GLORT
...TA QUADRANT
...PLANET IX
...RGAL

FNARG THE GREAT AND WISE
7120 XEN...
...LANE
...LANET 8

AVING A GREAT
E WISH YOU
AND WERE HERE.
HE 12 SUNS OF
AVE REALLY SINGED
AN'S VERTABRAE.

CARL: 17TH EARL
TO BORAN PERIMETRE
BLOXOR XII.
136 GRODAN CRES

It's a long flight to the edge of the universe, and even a genuine intergalactic space hero like Zack Proton needs a potty stop along the way, so Zack set the ship on autopilot, hopped out of his commander's chair on the bridge, and headed for his other commander's chair at the back of the ship.

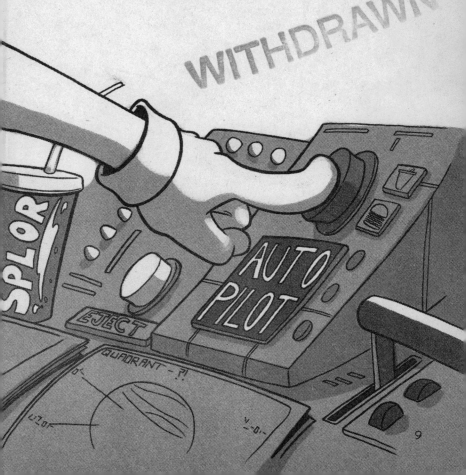

At the rear of the *Risky Rascal* were
two doors.

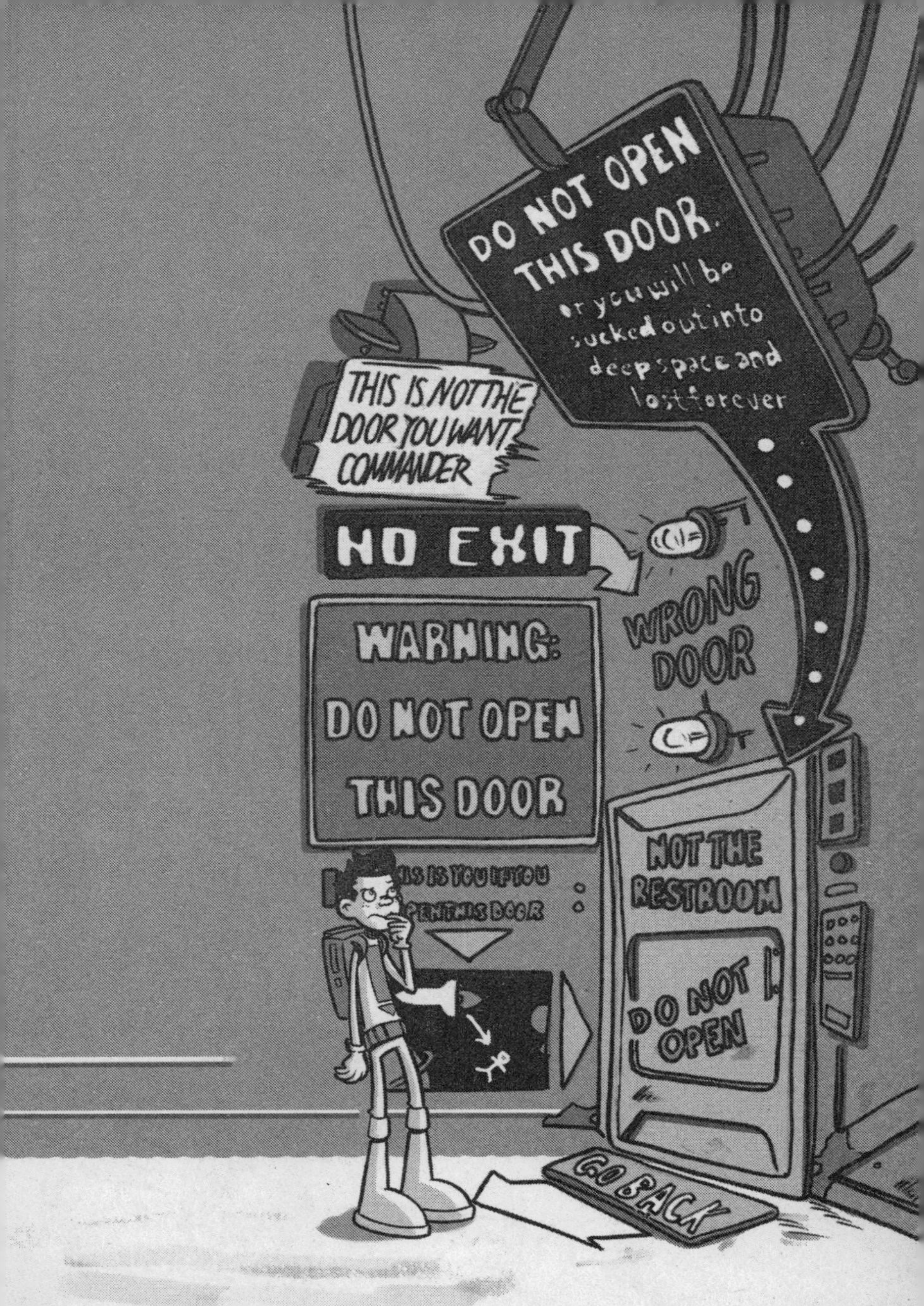
DO NOT OPEN THIS DOOR.
or you will be sucked out into deep space and lost forever
THIS IS NOT THE DOOR YOU WANT COMMANDER
NO EXIT
WRONG DOOR
WARNING: DO NOT OPEN THIS DOOR
NOT THE RESTROOM
DO NOT OPEN
GO BACK

Unfortunately, Commander Proton failed to notice the flashing lights and warning signs, and opened the wrong door.

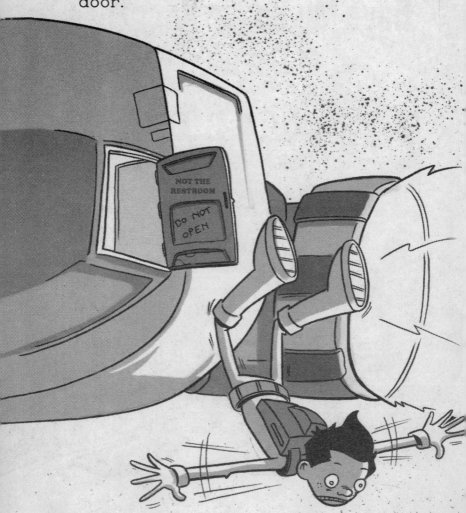

CHAPTER TWO

Oh Where, Oh Where Have My Space Rangers Gone?

Zack tumbled helplessly through space as his starship zoomed off without him. When he finally came to a stop, he took one look at the endless starry blackness surrounding him and quickly realized that something was not right.

"Leapin' leptons!" he cried. "My rest-room is getting away!"

Zack's starship was zipping through space at a speed of ninety-three thousand miles per second, and was now nothing more than a teeny tiny speck of red light in the distance.

Zack immediately started dog-paddling after his ship. Unfortunately, the *Risky Rascal* was traveling at half the speed of light, while Zack was barely inching along at all. He tried running in space. He tried the backstroke. He swam until he was exhausted. But it was no use.

By now even the teeny tiny speck of red light was gone, and Commander Zack Proton was all alone in outer space. Separated from his ship. Separated from his crew. He knew in an instant what this meant.

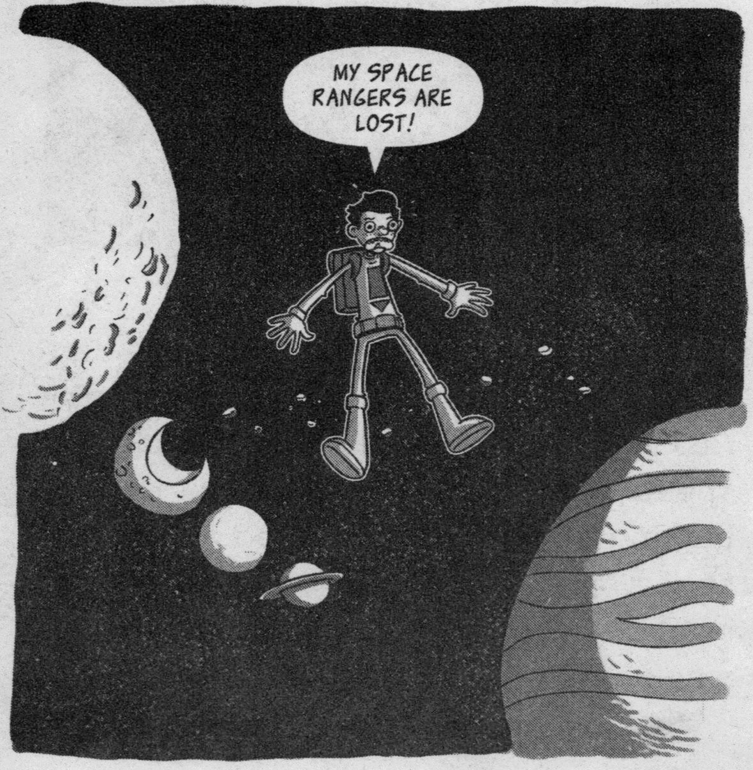
MY SPACE RANGERS ARE LOST!

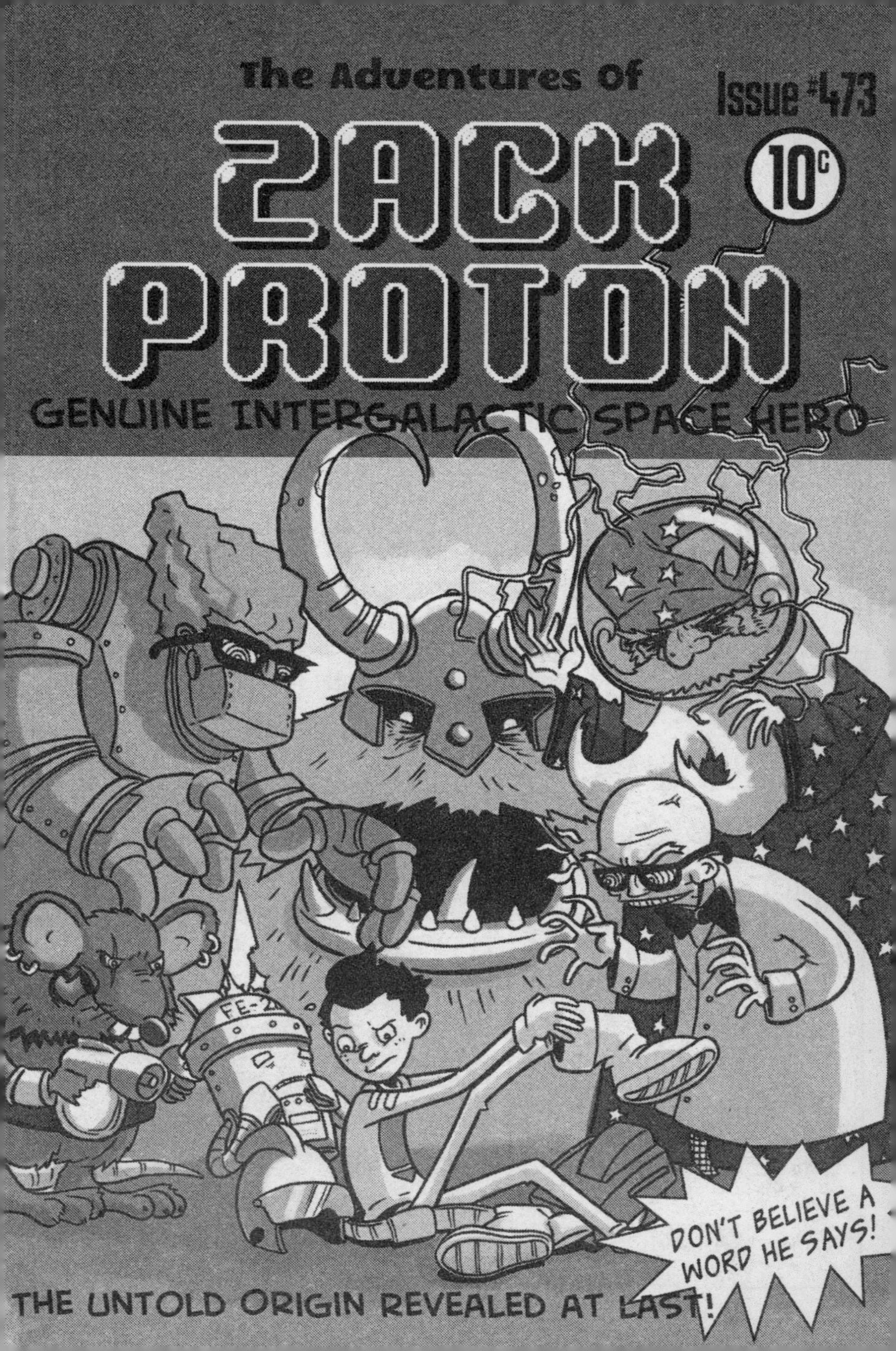
The Adventures of
ZACK PROTON
Issue #473
10¢
GENUINE INTERGALACTIC SPACE HERO
FE-2
DON'T BELIEVE A WORD HE SAYS!
THE UNTOLD ORIGIN REVEALED AT LAST!

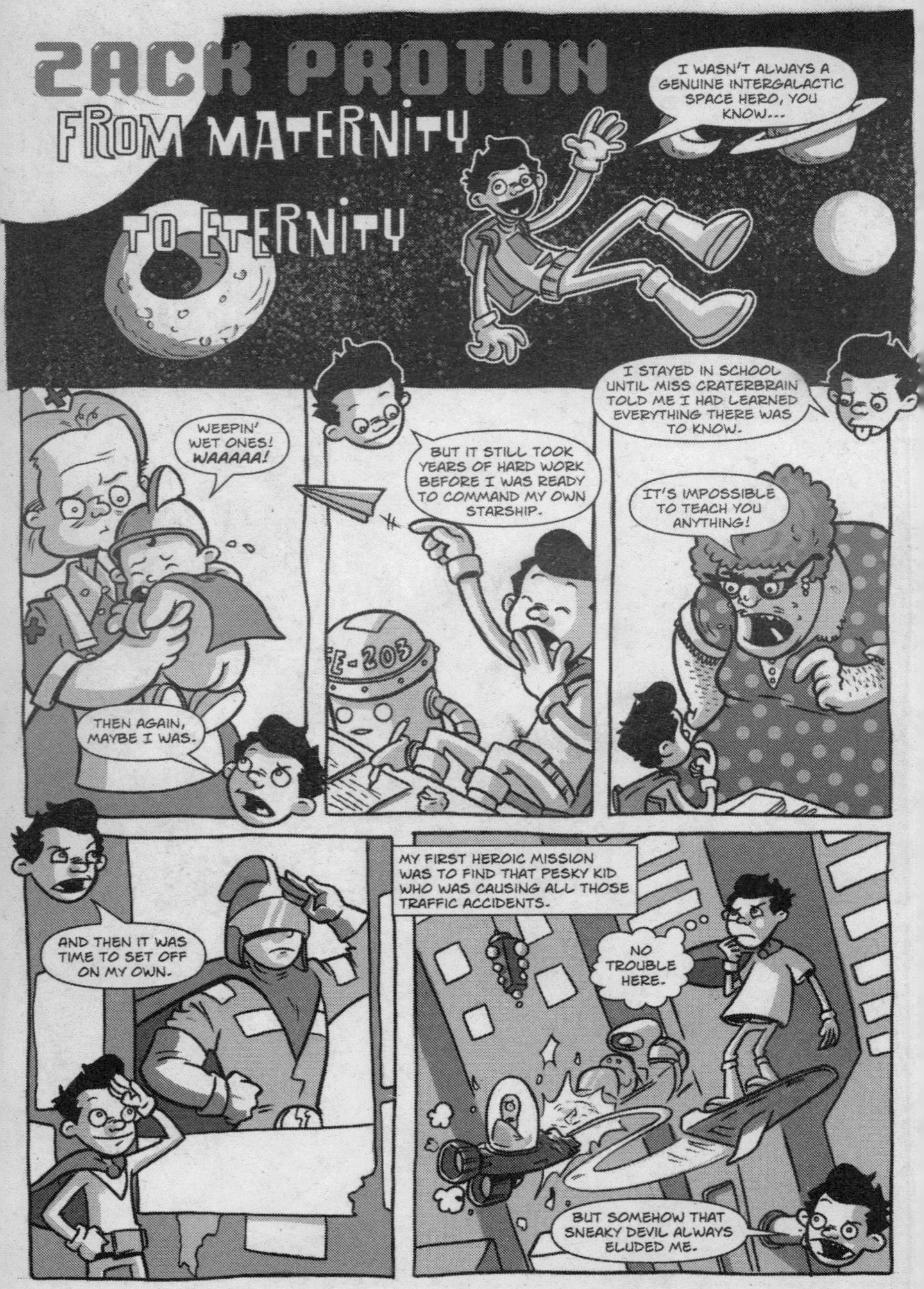
ZACK PROTON
FROM MATERNITY TO ETERNITY
I WASN'T ALWAYS A GENUINE INTERGALACTIC SPACE HERO, YOU KNOW...
WEEPIN' WET ONES! WAAAAA!
THEN AGAIN, MAYBE I WAS.
BUT IT STILL TOOK YEARS OF HARD WORK BEFORE I WAS READY TO COMMAND MY OWN STARSHIP.
E-203
I STAYED IN SCHOOL UNTIL MISS CRATERBRAIN TOLD ME I HAD LEARNED EVERYTHING THERE WAS TO KNOW.
IT'S IMPOSSIBLE TO TEACH YOU ANYTHING!
AND THEN IT WAS TIME TO SET OFF ON MY OWN.
MY FIRST HEROIC MISSION WAS TO FIND THAT PESKY KID WHO WAS CAUSING ALL THOSE TRAFFIC ACCIDENTS.
NO TROUBLE HERE.
BUT SOMEHOW THAT SNEAKY DEVIL ALWAYS ELUDED ME.

THEN I SAW THE JOB LISTING THAT WOULD CHANGE MY LIFE FOREVER.

GASP

ARE YOU FEARLESS, HEROIC, AND DARING?

YOU'RE *HIRED!*

I PUT THE *FOOL* IN FOOLHARDY! I PUT THE *STUPE* IN STUPENDOUS AND THE *PID* IN INTREPID!

TAKE *THAT*, YOU SLITHERING SPACE SLIME, YOU WIGGLING *WARP* WORMS!

I COULDN'T *WAIT* TO GET STARTED!

BUT MY FIRST ASSIGNMENT NEARLY ENDED MY CAREER.

I'M A **SPACE** HERO, NOT A **MAILMAN!**

DO IT OR YOU'RE **FIRED.**

NEITHER **RAIN** NOR **SLEET** NOR **COSMIC RAYS...**

WOOF!

I QUICKLY LEARNED THAT DELIVERING THE MAIL WAS NO WALK THOUGH THE SPACE PARK. DOWN BOYS! **DOWN!**

WOOF!

WOOF!

AND FOR A GENUINE INTERGALACTIC SPACE HERO LIKE ME, UNEXPECTED DANGERS LURK AT EVERY TURN.

WHOOPS, GOTTA GO. THEY NEED ME IN THE STORY NOW.

BUMP

CHAPTER THREE

An Unexpected Primate

Zack studied the stars around him to try to figure out precisely where he was, but didn't recognize any of the strange constellations glinting in the darkness.

Some people who find themselves hopelessly lost in outer space start to panic, or cry their wimpy little eyes out and fill their space helmets with tears. Others might foolishly waste their final hours with some pointless activity like counting stars. But Commander Zack Proton was a genuine intergalactic space hero and wasn't about to cry or panic over something as simple as certain death. Instead, he put his mind to work, starting with that big star on the left: "One, two, three, four . . ."

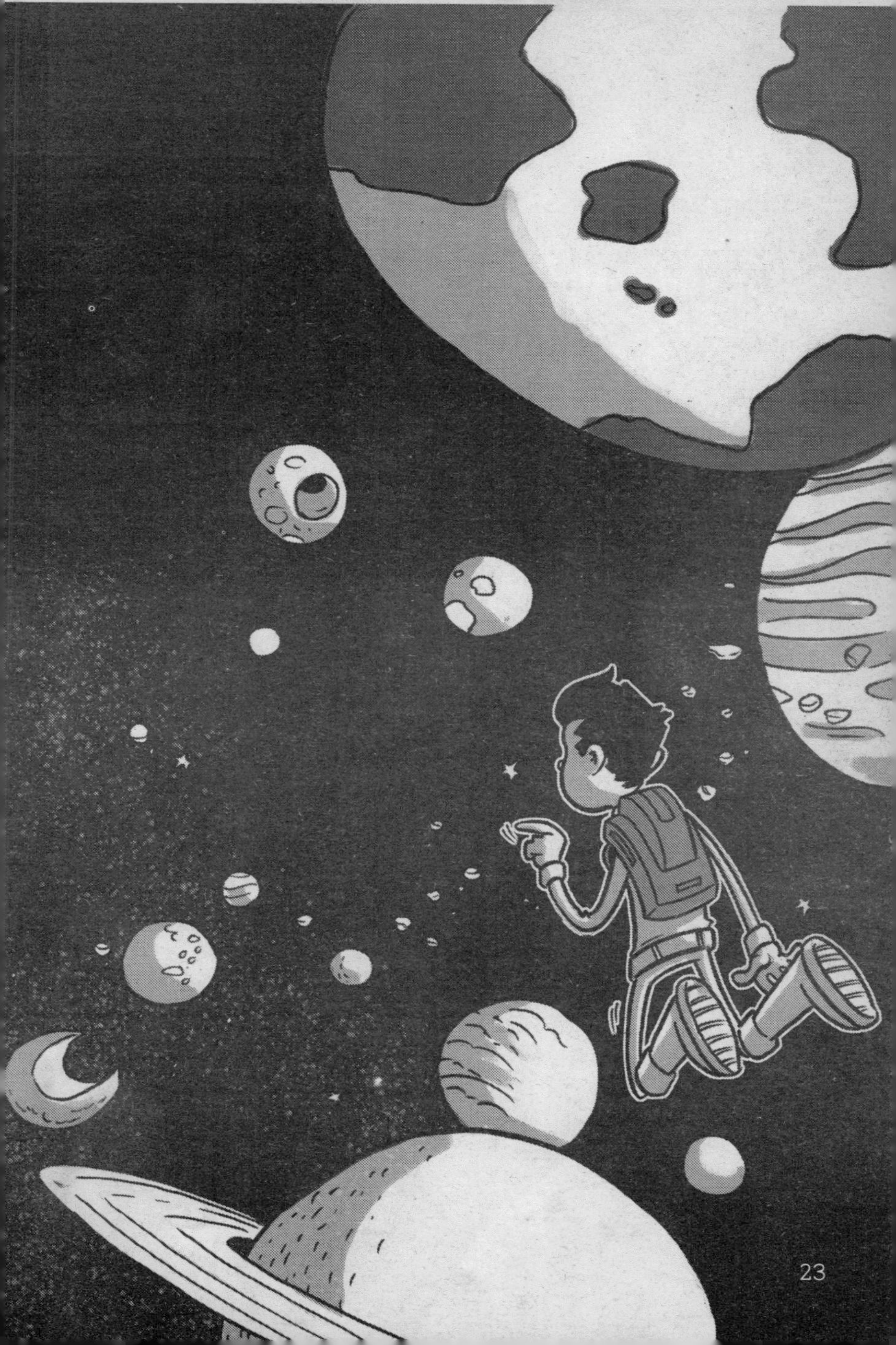

By the time he reached one thousand, Zack had counted some stars
twice and one star three times. But
when you're staring at billions and billions
of stars, mistakes like that are easy to
make.

"One thousand, six hundred and
twelve, one thousand six hundred and
fourteen . . ."

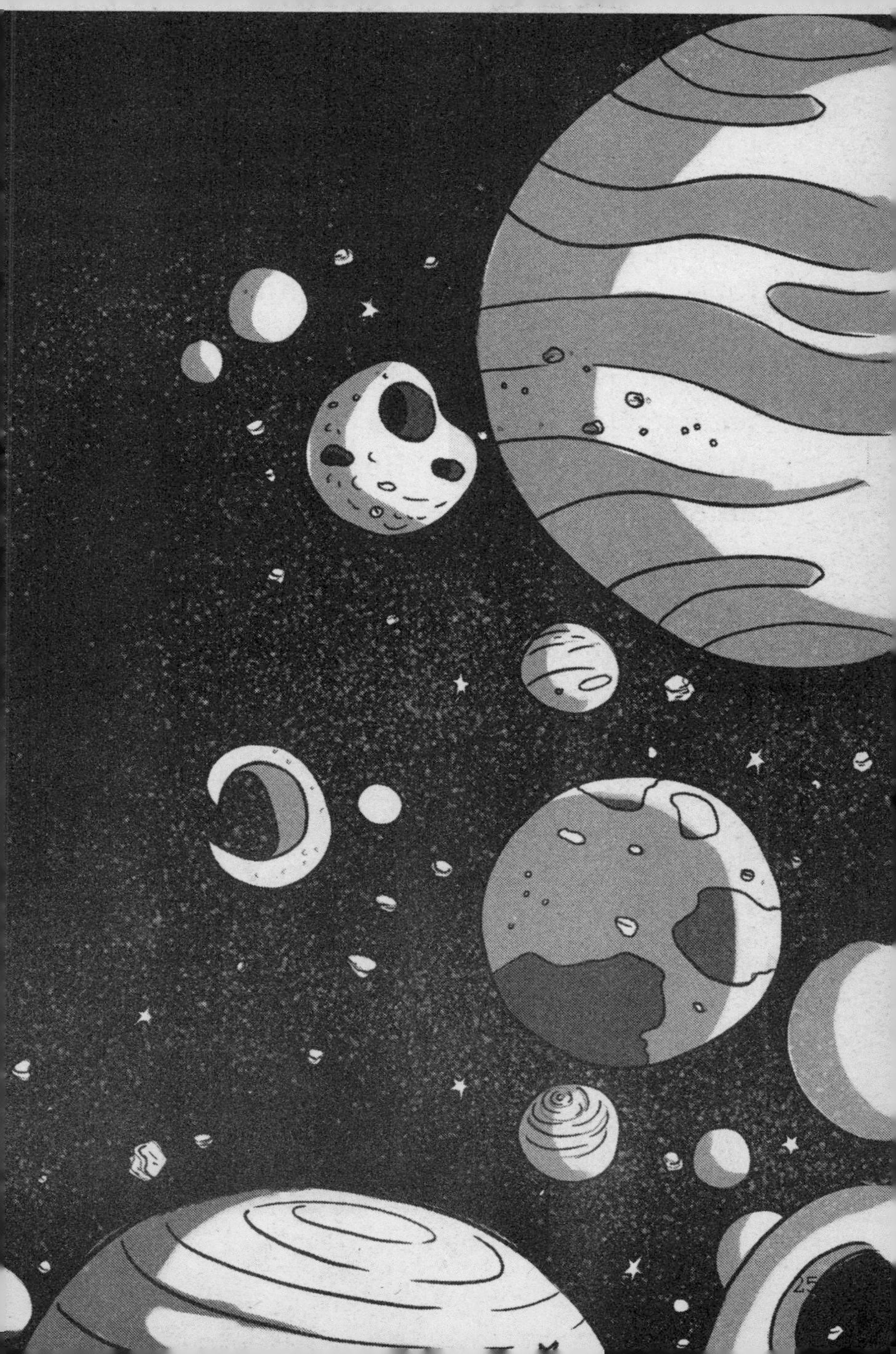

Zack felt a sudden bump from be-hind, and found himself pressed against the windshield of a small spacecraft.

"Hey, earthling! Get off the glass be-fore I crash into something," came a voice from within the spacecraft.

"You just *did* crash into something," Zack called back. "One thousand eight hundred and fifteen." He turned and gave an annoyed glance at the ship's pilot.

"Leapin' leptons!" he cried, "You're a monkey! An animal astronaut, a simian spaceman—"

"I'm a chimpanzee," said the pilot.

"I was getting there," Zack replied.

Zack stared in disbelief at the chimpanzee in the silver space suit. It was a real, live chimpanzee all right. He even had a half-eaten banana in his hand.

Zack gazed past the chimp to the rest of the ship. At the rear of the ship he saw two doors. The one on the left was marked RESTROOM.

Zack tapped urgently on the windshield. "Um, excuse me. . . ."

CHAPTER FOUR

How Do You Spell Relief?

Zack felt light-years better as he emerged from the restroom.

"Say, I noticed there's no name on your spaceship," Zack said to the chimp. "You can't call yourself a genuine inter-galactic space hero if your ship doesn't even have a name."

"I'm not a space hero, I'm a chimpanzee," the pilot said, taking another bite of banana to prove his point.

"Well, I am a space hero," Zack replied, "Commander Zack Proton to be exact. Captain of the *Risky Rascal*, commander of the Space Ranger Star Patrol."

"Omega Chimp," said the pilot, "the last chimpanzee ever sent into space—and then left there."

"Abandoned in space? Ooh, that's cold."

"Absolute zero," Omega Chimp answered.

"Well, let's just radio down to Earth, tell them Zack Proton is on board, and . . ." Zack looked over the cockpit controls, but something was missing. "Where's your radio?" he asked.

Omega Chimp finished chewing his banana and swallowed. "Don't have one," he said. "I took it apart and used the pieces to build myself a banana generator."

"You get your bananas from . . . that thing?"

"You see any banana trees on this ship?"

Zack was silent for a moment. His space rangers were still lost somewhere on the frayed fringes of the cosmos, alone and frightened without him. If only he had some way to reach them. If only he had a radio. If only he had a—

"Banana?" offered Omega Chimp.

"You read my mind!"

CHAPTER FIVE

We're Off to Save the Rangers

One banana later, Zack explained to Omega Chimp that his loyal space rangers were lost somewhere in the great inky blackness of space. "What we need right now is a genuine intergalactic space hero to save my squadron, to comfort my crew, to—"

"I already told you, I'm not a space hero," said Omega Chimp.

"I know," replied Zack. "I was talking about me. So what do you say, Omega Chimp? Will you brave the uncertain dangers of deep space and take me to the edge of the universe? Will you boldly go where no chimp has gone before? Will you help me find the *Risky Rascal*?"

"If I do, will you get off my ship?" Omega Chimp asked.

"Space hero's honor."

"Then let's not waste another second!"

Omega Chimp's Top Ten Ways to Get an Unwanted Space Hero Off Your Ship:

10. ~~Activate ship's self-destruct sequence.~~
    BAD IDEA

9. Announce over the ship's speakers that the last one off the ship is a monkey's uncle.

8. Tell him a meteor shower is approaching and ask him to step outside to see if it's raining.

7. Tell him you're allergic to heroes and fake a violent sneezing fit.

6 ~~Tell him heroes make you nauseous and . . .~~ BAD IDEA

5 Pretend you only speak chimp, and give him lots of big, toothy chimpanzee smiles.

4. Spray the entire ship with Zap 'Em Dead Ant and Space-Hero Killer.

3. Sing banana boat songs all day long.

2. Invite him to pick the fleas from your fur and eat them.

1. Wait for him to go to the bathroom and hope he opens the wrong door.

CHAPTER SIX

A Planet in Peril

Omega Chimp's ship set out at top speed, following the course the *Risky Rascal* had taken. At least, they thought they were following the *Risky Rascal*, but Omega Chimp wasn't so sure. When he had asked Zack for the *Risky Rascal*'s space coordinates, Zack just pointed and said, "They went thataway."

And so, thataway they went. Commander Proton scooped up an armload of bananas from the generator and settled down in the cockpit for a fruity feast, a banana buffet, a—

Beep! Beep! Beep! A blue light on the control panel flashed as Omega Chimp's ship picked up a distress signal.

"Why do they always call when I'm eating?" Zack grumbled through a mouthful of banana.

"It's a class 1-A distress signal," Omega Chimp said, studying the ship's computer monitor. "An entire planet in danger of immediate destruction."

"Leapin' leptons! We've got to save that planet!"

The distress call had come from planet Potluck, only two stars away, and it wasn't long before Omega Chimp's ship was orbiting the planet.

Omega Chimp checked his ship's control panel to see what the problem was.

"That's strange," he said. "My sensors aren't picking up any trouble at all. There's not so much as a bad haircut on the entire planet. I wonder what the problem is."

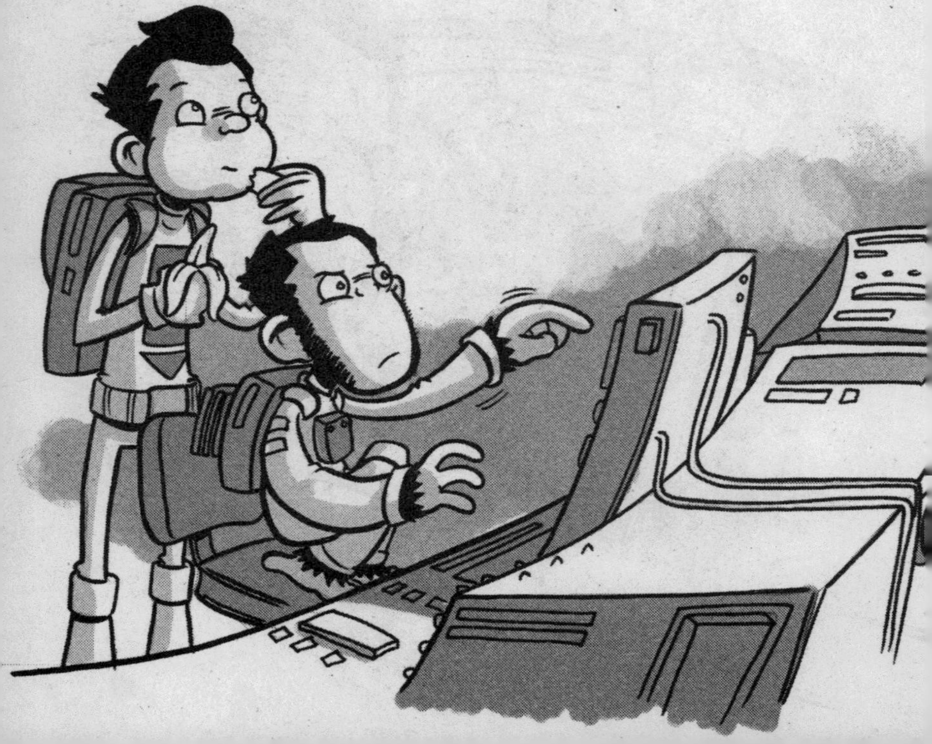

WARS: 0
EARTHQUAKES: 0
VOLCANOES: 0
MUDSLIDES: 0
HURRICANES: 0
BLIZZARDS: 0
MATH TESTS: 0

41

Maybe it has something to do with that," said Zack, pointing out the windshield.

CHAPTER SEVEN

One Orbiting Death Ray Can Ruin Your Whole Day

Zack laughed. "They sent out a distress signal over a silly little death ray? They must be a planet full of chicken-chested spaghetti-spines."

"This should make them feel better," Omega Chimp said as he jabbed a button on the control panel. A yellow light flashed, and a computer voice said, "Torpedo armed. Fire when ready."

"You've got quantum torpedoes!" Zack blurted out in surprise.

"I built them with the leftover parts from my landing rockets," Omega Chimp explained, as he pressed the fire button. The quantum torpedo tore

a streak of light through the darkness,
and the orbiting death machine exploded
in a swirling ball of nuclear fire.

Seconds later the massive churning fireball had burned itself out, and the stars twinkled peacefully over planet Potluck. *Beep! Beep! Beep!* The distress signal continued.

"They must have seen the light from that explosion," said Zack. "Why are they still sending out a distress signal?"

Beep! Bee-bee-beep! Beep-beep-beeeeep!

"Wait, the signal's changing," said Omega Chimp. "They're sending a coded message!"

Omega Chimp grabbed a pencil and paper and started translating:

"We're . . . not . . . afraid . . . of . . . a . . . silly . . . little . . . death . . . ray. We're . . . afraid . . . of . . . big . . . large. . . ."

"Big Large!" cried Zack Proton in horror.

"Big large what?" Omega Chimp asked.

Just then an enormous hand closed around Omega Chimp's ship. Zack and Omega Chimp felt their ship being lifted through space, until they found themselves staring face to face with the evilest, nastiest, most horriblest space giant ever to walk the spaceways—Big Large!

CHAPTER EIGHT

Two for Lunch?

Big Large was so enormous he devoured entire planets for breakfast. He stomped his way rudely through space, crushing comets and moons and asteroids as he searched for delicious crunchy-lunchy planets full of juicy-sweet creatures to eat. Planets exactly like Potluck.

Big La was here

Big Large had a thick red beard and wore a suit of gleaming metal armor with heavy boots, spiked gauntlets, and a fearsome helmet that covered everything except his big, bulging, angry eyes. Right now those two eyeballs stared murderously at Zack and Omega Chimp.

"We're goners, Omega Chimp," Zack said. "Appetizers before the main course. Me, the second greatest space hero in the universe, reduced to nothing more than a noontime nibble for that mammoth menace, a crunchy treat for that colossal troll, a—"

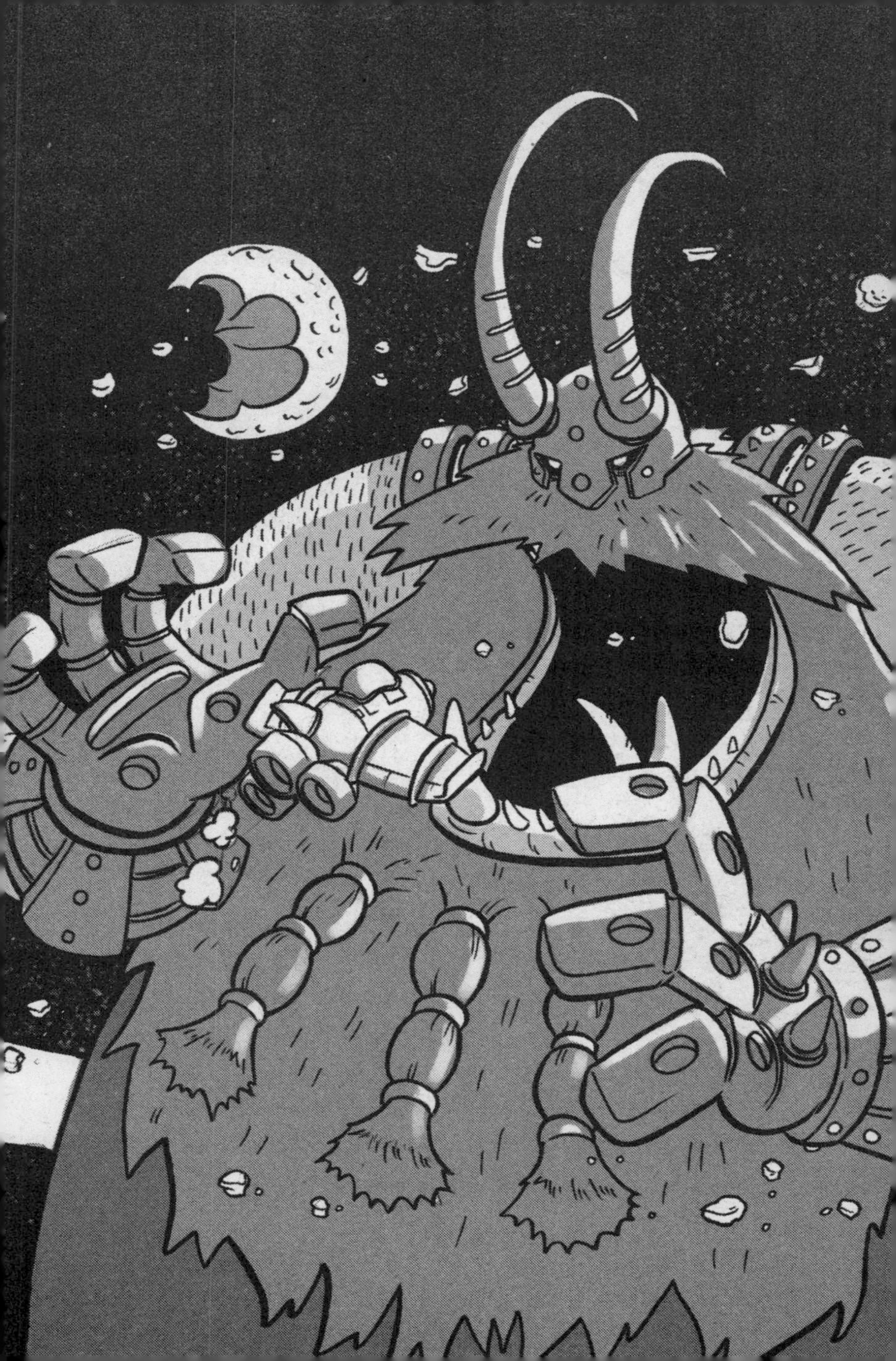

"Torpedo armed. Fire when ready," the computer interrupted.

Omega Chimp punched the fire button, and a quantum torpedo shot out from the ship and exploded right in Big Large's face.

Zack Proton pumped a fist. "Oh yeah! Right between the eyes! That'll teach him to mess with Commander Zack Proton!"

ZACK PROTON'S TIPS FOR YOUNG SPACE HEROES

Tip #1: No problem is so large that it can't be solved with a quantum torpedo.

The cloud of fire and smoke cleared, and Big Large glared at them, his bulging eyes fuming with rage.

"I don't think you should have done that," Zack said.

ZACK PROTON'S TIPS FOR YOUNG SPACE HEROES

Tip #2: Forget what I said about the quantum torpedo.

CHAPTER NINE

Shaken, Not Stirred

Big Large shook the spaceship up and down, back and forth, and up and down some more. Inside the ship, Zack Proton, Omega Chimp, and a half ton of bananas were tossed around like fruit salad in a cafeteria food fight.

"He's bruising my bananas!" Omega Chimp shouted, crashing into the ceiling.

"He's bruising *me*!" Zack shouted back, whacking a wall.

"You'll heal!"

"They'll peel!"

"I'm serious!"

"So am I!"

The shaking suddenly stopped, and everything came to a rest inside the ship.

"I feel as flat as one of my mother's banana pancakes," Omega Chimp moaned.

"I'm just glad that's over," said Zack.

But outside the ship, Big Large curled his index finger against his thumb, and . . .

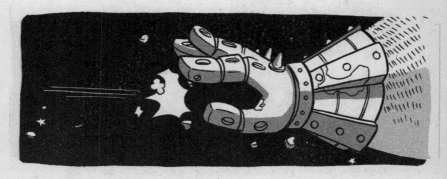

. . . *thwack!* sent the ship spiraling backward through space at a million miles per hour.

TANGANYIKA JANE'S FAMOUS BANANA PANCAKES

THAT'S MY BOY. HE'S AN ASTRONAUT YOU KNOW.

JUST LIKE MOM USED TO MAKE!

INGREDIENTS

1 CUP FLOUR
1 EGG, BEATEN
1 TABLESPOON SUGAR
1 CUP MILK
2 TEASPOONS BAKING POWDER
2 TABLESPOONS VEGETABLE OIL
1/4 TEASPOONS SALT
2 BANANAS, MASHED

STEP 1 —
COMBINE THE FLOUR, SUGAR, BAKING POWDER, AND SALT IN A HOLLOWED—OUT COCONUT SHELL. (IF YOU DON'T HAVE ANY COCONUTS, A PLASTIC BOWL WILL DO.)

STEP 2 —
PEEL THE BANANAS (DUH!) AND MASH THEM
WITH A FORK IF YOUR MOM IS THERE, OR WITH
YOUR HANDS IF SHE'S NOT.
IT WON'T LOOK VERY
TASTY WHEN YOU'RE
DONE, BUT DON'T WORRY
–– YOU USED TO LOVE THIS
STUFF WHEN YOU WERE A BABY.

STEP 3 —
MIX THE MILK, EGG, VEGETABLE
OIL, AND BANANA MUSH IN
ANOTHER COCONUT SHELL.

STIR THE FLOUR MIXTURE
INTO THE BANANA MIXTURE.
THE BATTER WILL BE LUMPY.

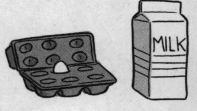

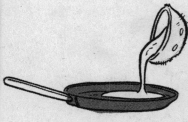

STEP 4 —
GET A GROWN-UP TO HELP WITH
THIS NEXT PART SO NO
PANCAKES OR FINGERS ARE
ACCIDENTALLY BURNED.

DROP STICKY GLOBS OF BATTER
ONTO A HOT FRYING PAN ONE BIG
DIPPERFUL AT A TIME, AND COOK
OVER MEDIUM-HIGH HEAT UNTIL
THE PANCAKES LOOK LIKE THE
LUNAR SURFACE. FLIP 'EM OVER
AND COOK 'EM FOR ABOUT A
MINUTE MORE, UNTIL BOTH SIDES
ARE THE GOLDEN BROWN COLOR
OF SATURN IN THE SPRINGTIME.

STEP 5 —
SERVE WITH MAPLE SYRUP OR SPRINKLE WITH
POWDERED SUGAR. FOR SOME EXTRA EARLY-
MORNING FUN, SPRINKLE WITH EXPLODING
PLUTONIAN BINKO SEEDS, SERVE QUICKLY, AND
RUN! FEEDS 6 CHIMPS.

"Omega Chimp?"

"Hm?"

"Can you get off me now?"

"As soon as I finish my breakfast."

CHAPTER TEN

An Unemployed Little Droid

Two hours and two million miles later, Omega Chimp finally managed to bring his tumbling ship under control. Bananas were everywhere, and Zack had a terrible case of space sickness that turned his face as green as an unripened banana.

Omega Chimp slowed the ship and began to orbit a frozen, lifeless planet on the outer edge of some unknown solar system.

"We're lost!" Zack Proton moaned. "Now I know how my poor space rangers must feel."

"We're not lost," Omega Chimp replied. "We're exactly where we want to be—two million miles away from Big Large. Soon to be three million."

"We have to go back!" Zack declared. "We haven't finished our battle with that clanking cosmic clod. Say, what's that?"

Outside their spaceship, a chunk of cold metal drifted slowly toward them. As it drew nearer, they could gradually make out a shape. Bigger than a bread-box, smaller than an ostrich, it looked like a chubby little fire hydrant.

"Leapin' leptons! That's an Effie-Two-Oh-Three!" Zack cried out. "A space droid! I had one of those when I was little!"

"Didn't they recall that model?" Omega Chimp asked. "If I remember right, they had all kinds of problems. . . ."

"Nonsense," said Zack. "Let's bring him aboard."

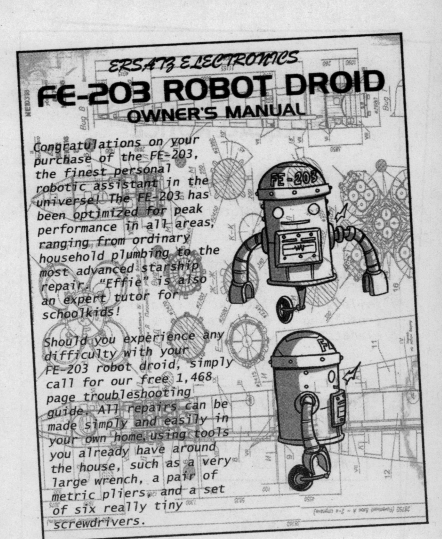

ERSATZ ELECTRONICS
FE-203 ROBOT DROID
OWNER'S MANUAL

Congratulations on your purchase of the FE-203, the finest personal robotic assistant in the universe! The FE-203 has been optimized for peak performance in all areas, ranging from ordinary household plumbing to the most advanced starship repair. "Effie" is also an expert tutor for schoolkids!

Should you experience any difficulty with your FE-203 robot droid, simply call for our free 1,468 page troubleshooting guide. All repairs can be made simply and easily in your own home, using tools you already have around the house, such as a very large wrench, a pair of metric pliers, and a set of six really tiny screwdrivers.

OFFICIAL GOVERNMENT RECALL NOTICE

Erzatx Electronic's Model FE-203 Robot Droid
If you are the unlucky owner of an FE-203, turn it off immediately and return it to the manufacturer for a full refund.

The FE-203 droid is dangerously defective and has been linked to fires, explosions, leaky toilets, exploding toilets, and toilets that flush up instead of down (resulting in widespread flooding on six planets).

WARNING: *The FE-203 is also responsible for countless failed math and spelling tests. Whatever you do, DO NOT let your FE-203 help your children with their homework!*

CHAPTER ELEVEN

If You Can't Beat 'Em . . .

Omega Chimp had a bad feeling about bringing the FE-203 on board, but he hoped that if Zack had a new toy to play with, he would forget about Big Large. Omega Chimp positioned his ship in front of the drifting droid, and the small robot floated into the ship's open storage bay with a loud *thunk*.

Zack opened the inner door to the storage bay, and the droid tumbled out and crashed to the floor. Sparks exploded from an electrical panel on its side and hundreds of tiny lights flashed randomly over its metal surface. "Error. Error. Error," a mechanical voice repeated.

"Don't worry, this is normal," Zack said. "Mine did this all the time. Quick—get me the biggest wrench you can find, a pair of metric pliers, and a set of six really tiny screwdrivers."

POP

Omega Chimp scoured the ship. He found the wrench and pliers immediately, but he could never remember where he put those six really tiny screwdrivers.

Omega Chimp finally found the screwdrivers, and gave all the tools to Zack. Zack grabbed the big wrench, raised it high above his head, and whacked the FE-203 right between the *F* and the *E*. The sparks stopped flying, and the little lights began flashing in a pattern. Two robotic arms extended from the sides of the space droid and pushed the FE-203 to a standing position.

"Thank you," said the droid's mechanical voice. "Effie-Two-Oh-Three at your service." A sudden burst of sparks erupted from the top of the droid.

"Good as new!" said Zack.

"You're done?" asked Omega Chimp. "But you never used the pliers or the six really tiny screwdrivers."

"Of course not," Zack replied. "I never used them on my old one either."

Omega Chimp pounded his head in frustration, but Zack had already turned toward FE-203. "Why's a nice droid like you orbiting a planet like this?"

Lights flashed on the FE-203 as he accessed his memory circuits. "The last thing I remember, I was doing repairs on my last owner's spaceship when we encountered a hideous red space giant."

"Big Large!" Zack cried.

"I don't know what happened next, but I woke up circling the planet below, and I've been orbiting ever since."

"You're in luck, Effie," Zack said. "We're on our way right now to battle that big bully, conquer that crimson cream puff, vanquish that vermilion villain!"

"No, we aren't," Omega Chimp said.

"This time I've got a plan," Zack said. "What do you say, Effie? Want to be a genuine intergalactic space hero like me?"

"Okay," Effie said.

"Two to one, you lose," Zack said to Omega Chimp. "Unless you're some kind of spineless spoilsport? A cowardly kill-joy? A pickle-pussed party pooper?"

"I am not a pickle-pussed party pooper!" Omega Chimp screamed.

"Then we're going back?" asked Zack.

Omega Chimp set the ship's controls to return to planet Potluck. "This is the stupidest thing I've ever done in my entire life," he grumbled.

"Spoken like a true space hero!" Zack said.

CHAPTER TWELVE

Yes, We Have No Bananas

The only thing worse than fighting an angry space giant was doing it on an empty stomach. So, Omega Chimp trudged to the back of the ship to grab some lunch. Since his entire banana supply had been badly bruised, he turned on his banana generator to make a new batch.

Nothing happened. No lights, no familiar humming sound, and worst of all, not one sweet, succulent, scrumptious burst of yellow delight emerged from the machine.

The banana generator was broken.

Omega Chimp's scream echoed throughout the ship.

Zack Proton and Effie rushed to the back of the ship. Omega Chimp was hugging his broken banana machine and crying his chimpie little eyes out.

"Bananaless!" he sobbed. "I'm banana-less in space forever!"

"Don't panic, Omega Chimp," Zack said. "Effie's a robotic genius. He'll fix your banana generator in no time."

"Banana?" Effie asked.

"Yeah, banana. You know." Zack grabbed a banana peel from the trash. He held it up for Effie to see. "Banana."

"Banana. Of course. No problem."
Seven robotic arms sprang out from
Effie's sides, each one of them armed
with a different tool. "Stand back," he
said.

THE **TOP-SECRET** CLASSIFIED
OMEGA CHIMP

**WARNING: DO NOT LEAK THIS INFORMATION TO ANYONE!
MAKE 'EM BUY THEIR OWN BOOK!**

IN THE DARKEST JUNGLES OF BORNEO...

CHIMPANZEES DON'T LIVE IN BORNEO!

IN THE DARKEST JUNGLES OF AFRICA...

I WAS BORN AT THE MILWAUKEE ZOO!

IN THE DARKEST JUNGLES OF MILWAUKEE, WISCONSIN...

WHY DO I BOTHER?

...A BABY CHIMP WAS BORN.

OOK OOK!

I NEVER DRESSED LIKE THAT!

ZIS *MISSION* IS TOO DANGEROUS FOR A HUMAN! VE NEED A *MONKEY!*

HOW 'BOUT THAT CUTE LITTLE FELLER IN PANEL 4?

HEY, WAIT A MINUTE!

THE PROGRESS OF SCIENCE DEMANDS IT!

OOK. OOK.

UNHAND THAT CHIMPLING!

THIS WAS THE BEGINNING OF MY TRAINING AS A SPACE MONKEY.

HOW CAN HE FLY THE SHIP IF HE CAN'T READ THE CONTROLS?

VE NEED TO *SPEECHIFY* ZIS BEAST!

AFTER ZIS HE VILL SCHPEEK *PERFECT* ENGLISH!

AFTER THIS YOU SHOULD TRY IT ON YOURSELF!

GET YOUR FILTHY HANDS *OFF* ME, YOU DARN DIRTY *HUMAN!*

IT *VORKED!*

CAN WE CHANGE HIM BACK NOW?

OOK OOK.

IT WASN'T LONG BEFORE I HAD COMPLETED MY MISSION AND WAS READY TO COME HOME.

WE'VE DECIDED TO LEAVE YOU UP THERE AND SPEND THE REST OF THE BUDGET ON A GIANT PIZZA PARTY.

PIZZA PARTY!!!

THEY WOULDN'T *DARE* PULL THAT ON BUZZ ALDRIN!

I NEVER *DID* CARE MUCH FOR PIZZA ANYWAY.

AND BEING ALL ALONE OUT HERE IN OUTER SPACE IS NICE AND PEACEFUL, AS LONG AS --

YOU'RE A *MONKEY!* AN *ANIMAL* ASTRONAUT, A SIMIAN *SPACEMAN*...

I MISS THE ZOO.

CHAPTER THIRTEEN

One Banana, Two Banana, Three Banana, Four

Zack and Omega Chimp listened to the buzzing and whirring of Effie's tools as he worked, along with the clinks, clanks, and clunks of pieces of the machine falling to the floor.

"He's not breaking it, is he?" Omega Chimp asked uncertainly.

"Trust me, by the time Effie's finished with it, your banana generator will work like never before," Zack answered.

Suddenly the noises came to an abrupt stop. Effie rolled forward. "All finished," he said. Behind him, Omega Chimp's banana generator gleamed like new.

"What'd I tell you?" Zack said. "Effie's a genius!"

"I made some improvements to your design," Effie said to Omega Chimp. "Your machine will now produce bananas a hundred times faster than before."

"A hundred times!"

"Go ahead, Omega Chimp," Zack said. "Start her up."

Omega Chimp flipped the on switch. The lights flickered, and a gentle humming started. Seconds later a familiar yellow shape flew out of the machine and landed smack on Omega Chimp's nose. Omega Chimp removed the peel from his face and gaped at it in bewilderment. "This isn't a banana," he said. "It's just a peel."

Suddenly the lights flashed faster, the machine began to shake, and the gentle humming grew into an angry roar. Banana peels began firing out of the machine by the hundreds.

"Redshift!" yelled Zack, but it was too late.

A solid stream of peels exploded from the banana generator. Peels flew everywhere. Zack and the others were lost in the slippery yellow blizzard.

"Turn it off!" Omega Chimp shouted through the storm.

Effie stabbed blindly at the machine until he finally found the off switch. The flashing lights went dark, the roaring dwindled to silence, and one last limp banana peel dropped out of the machine.

Zack turned to Omega Chimp. "Well, except for not making the banana part, I'd say Effie did a great job, wouldn't you?"

"Get him off my ship!" Omega Chimp screamed.

Effie's lights all turned blue.

Just then an alert sounded in the cockpit.

They had reached their destination.
Out the window, Big Large was reaching for the planet Potluck with a very
hungry look in his eyes.

THE ZZZZZZAQ FAQ!

Readers' questions answered by the second-greatest genuine intergalactic space hero of all time.

Q: Isn't "redshift" the term astronomers use when objects quickly moving away appear to turn red in color? So when you say "redshift!" isn't that just a cowardly way of saying "Run away!"?

A: Absolutely not. "Redshift!" is a very heroic way of saying "Run away!"

Q: When are you going to get off my ship?

A: Sorry, Omega Chimp. This page is for readers only.

Q: Isn't a red giant a type of star?

A: Yes, and I'm glad you asked. There are many different types of stars in the universe....

GRATUITOUS EDUCATIONAL CONTENT OBLITERATED

Q: When are you going to get off Omega Chimp's ship? Signed, A. Reader, Milwaukee, Wisconsin

A: Nice try, Omega Chimp, but I know it's you.

Q: What is a leapin' lepton, anyway?

A: Excellent question! Leptons are a class of subatomic particles which... [Editor's note: 37 pages of rambling pseudoscientific poppycock deleted.] I hope that answers your question!

Thanks for writing, and keep those
questions coming!
(Not you, Omega Chimp.)
See you next time!

CHAPTER FOURTEEN

My Kingdom for a Quantum Torpedo

"**H**e's about to eat Potluck for dinner!" cried Omega Chimp as he raced his ship toward Big Large. "Quick! What's your plan?"

ZACK PROTON'S TIPS FOR YOUNG SPACE HEROES

Tip #3: Forget what I said when I said forget what I said about the quantum torpedo.

"It's easy," Zack said. "Sneak up behind him, fire two quantum torpedoes right into those big sweaty armpits of his, and *boom*! Game over. Commander Zack Proton wins again!"

"We don't have any quantum torpedoes," Omega Chimp said.

"Of course we do. You shot off two of them already."

"Those were the only two I had."

"Leapin' leptons! You should have told me we don't have any more torpedoes!" Zack screamed.

"You never said you needed them!" Omega Chimp screamed back.

ZACK PROTON'S TIPS FOR YOUNG SPACE HEROES

Tip #4: You can't solve any size problem with a quantum torpedo unless you actually have a quantum torpedo.

"Hey guys? I think he sees us." said Effie.

Big Large glared at them with those two angry, bulging eyes, madder than ever. Ignoring the planet, he reached for their ship instead.

CHAPTER FIFTEEN

Six Banana, Seven Banana, Eight Banana, More!

"Redshift!" Zack Proton screamed as their ship fled from the furious red giant.

"I'm trying!" Omega Chimp shouted.

"He's gaining," Effie said. "Do something!"

Omega Chimp frantically searched the control panel for any kind of weapon, but the quantum torpedoes were gone, and his ship was completely helpless. The closest thing he had to a weapon was the big landing light on the back of the ship.

"Effie," Omega Chimp called, "go to the back of the ship and aim the spotlight at Big Large. I'll try to blind him with a bright flash of light."

Effie rolled to the back of the ship and pulled on the spotlight control stick. It snapped off in his hand. He glanced out the back window at the spotlight, which was now aimed at him instead of at Big Large.

At that moment Omega Chimp threw a switch, and a powerful flash of white light went off at the rear of the ship.

"Did it work?" called Omega Chimp.

"Well, yes and no . . . ," Effie answered, stumbling around blindly. Effie bashed into a wall and fell against the banana generator.

"He's closing in on us!" Zack shouted.

"We can't go any faster," Omega Chimp cried. "The ship is too heavy."

Effie grabbed the top of the banana generator to pull himself up, and accidentally turned it on. The shaking and roaring started immediately. Thick swarms of banana peels flew through the air and fell by the thousands in massive heaps all over the floor, adding even more weight to the ship.

"We're slowing down!" Omega Chimp screamed.

Through the open cockpit door, Zack saw the ship filling up with banana peels.

"We're going to be flattened by fruit," Zack cried, "buried in bananas, plastered with peels!"

Zack Proton and Omega Chimp slammed the cockpit door and held it closed against the push of banana peels. The door bulged toward them as the pressure from the banana peels increased, and it took all their strength to hold it shut.

Suddenly Zack cried out in alarm. "Flaming nuclear death at twelve o'clock!"

Omega Chimp looked out the windshield. While they were busy holding the cockpit door, the ship had veered off course. They were headed directly toward the planet's sun!

CHAPTER SIXTEEN

A Whole Bunch of Trouble

"**W**arning," said the computerized control panel voice. "Impact with star in twenty seconds."

NINETEEN, EIGHTEEN, SEVENTEEN...

"I've got to turn the ship!" cried Omega Chimp. "But if I let go of the door, we'll be crushed by banana peels!"

"Don't worry about the sun," said Zack. "Big Large is sure to catch us before we get that far."

"Is that supposed to cheer me up?" Omega Chimp cried. Suddenly Effie called from the back of the ship, "Big Large is here! He's reaching for us!"

"See? I told you!" Zack said.

"We're all going to die!" Omega Chimp wailed.

CHAPTER SEVENTEEN

And into the Fire

"Ten, nine, eight . . ." The computer countdown continued.

"I don't want to be a genuine inter-space hero anymore!" Effie squealed from the back of the ship.

Go hide in the bathroom if you're scared," Zack shouted back to him. "It's the door on your right."

"No, on your left!" shouted Omega Chimp, but he was too late. Effie reached out with a mechanical arm and turned the knob on the right. The back door of the spaceship opened, and ten million banana peels spilled out into space.

Big Large hit the peels at full speed. His feet spun wildly in circles beneath him, and his arms waved at his sides as he tried to regain his balance. The raging banana generator spewed out a

million more banana peels in front of Big Large as Omega Chimp's ship sped straight toward the sun.

In the cockpit Omega Chimp leaped for the controls. He turned the ship safely away from the sun, but Big Large, still slipping and sliding and dancing through space on a gigantic banana peel sidewalk, couldn't stop. Arms and legs flailing, and banana peels flying everywhere, Big Large followed the slippery trail directly toward the sun until he crashed with a bright fiery explosion into the surface of the star.

"Leapin' leptons!" Zack cried out, "We did it, Omega Chimp! We beat Big Large!"

"Planet Potluck to unidentified space vessel," said a radio voice from a speaker on Effie's side. "Come in, please."

"You've got a radio!" cried Omega Chimp. "You should have told me you had a radio!"

"You never said you needed one," Effie replied.

Which Effie isn't like the others?

CHAPTER EIGHTEEN

A Potluck Banquet

The grateful inhabitants of planet Potluck threw a planetwide dinner party to celebrate their victory over Big Large. For dessert the waiters brought out the biggest, freshest banana splits Zack had ever seen.

"Leapin' leptons! Lemme at it!" Zack snatched up his bowl so fast the dessert spilled out and plopped onto the floor. Zack's banana split was now a banana *splat*.

Fortunately, the waiter arrived with a fresh dessert just in time.

"Psst! Real space heroes don't eat off the floor," the waiter whispered.

"I knew that," Zack replied, getting up quickly.

While the three heroes were enjoying their rewards, an expert team of rocket scientists and repairmen was hard at work on Omega Chimp's spaceship. Besides fixing the banana generator, they also replaced the missing landing gear, installed a brand new radio, and made a few other upgrades and improvements as well.

"What kind of improvements?" Omega Chimp asked.

"Why don't we show you," a repairman replied.

Zack, Effie, and Omega Chimp were taken to the spaceport where Omega Chimp's ship was waiting. The first thing they noticed was the fresh coat of paint, with a name written along the side of the ship: *Giant Slayer*.

"We hope you don't mind," said one of the repairmen. "But you can't call yourself a genuine intergalactic space hero if your ship doesn't even have a name."

"Told you so," added Zack.

"Giant Slayer . . . I like it," Omega Chimp said with a smile.

"Congratulations!" cried Zack. "Now you're a real space hero like me!"

"Like us!" Effie corrected him.

"Well, maybe not *exactly* like you," Omega Chimp began, and decided to leave it at that.

CHAPTER NINETEEN

A Sty in the Sky

"**W**e're really sorry about littering up your solar system with all those banana peels," Omega Chimp told the repairmen.

"Oh, they're all gone," one of the repairmen answered. "A ship carrying sixteen million pigs came by and swept them all up. You need a lot of slop when you're taking that many pigs all the way across the universe."

"Sixteen million pigs! They'll never get the smell out of their ship." Zack laughed. "What kind of nutty starship captain would take a job like that?"

"They don't have a captain. They said he fell out the back door of the ship, and they've been crisscrossing the universe looking for him ever since."

"The *Risky Rascal*!" cried Zack.

"You've heard of it?"

"Leapin' leptons, that's my ship! Quick—what was their bearing?"

"They went thataway," a repairman said.

"Follow those pigs!" screamed Zack. The repairmen all scrambled out the back door of the ship as Zack hit the gas. The engines kicked on, and the ship rose up smoothly into the skies over Potluck.

"We've got to rescue my rangers, save my spacemen," Zack said. "We've got to . . . um . . ."

"Pursue those pork chops?" Omega Chimp suggested.

"Pursue those pork chops!" Zack shouted.

And with that, the *Giant Slayer* zoomed off thataway into space.

The End

WANTED

$250,000 REWARD

ELVIS EINSTEIN ERSATZ, DOCTOR OF ROBOTICS

FORMER OWNER OF THE NOW DEFUNCT ERSATZ ELECTRONICS, MAKER OF THE FE-203 PERSONAL ASSISTANT ROBOT DROID.

DR. ERSATZ DISAPPEARED WITH OVER 10,000 DEFECTIVE ROBOTS AND NEVER ISSUED REFUNDS TO THEIR OWNERS.

WARNING: DR. ERSATZ IS AN INSANE GENIUS AND SHOULD BE CONSIDERED BIZARRE AND DANGEROUS.

IF YOU SEE HIM, NOTIFY YOUR LOCAL INTERGALACTIC LAW ENFORCEMENT AGENCY IMMEDIATELY. DO NOT APPROACH HIM YOURSELF UNLESS YOU ARE A *GENUINE INTERGALACTIC SPACE HERO!*